MARGARET CLARK

Cocky Too

AUSSIE ANGELS 6

Mark Macleod BOOKS
Hodder Headline Australia

A Mark Macleod Book

Published in Australia and New Zealand in 2000
by Hodder Headline Australia Pty Limited,
(A member of the Hodder Headline Group)
Level 22, 201 Kent Street, Sydney NSW 2000
Website: www.hha.com.au

National Library of Australia
Cataloguing-in-Publication data

Clark, M. D. (Margaret Dianne), 1943- .
  Cocky Too.

  ISBN 0 7336 1210 5.

  1. Cockatoos - Juvenile fiction. I. Title. (Series: Clark, M. D.
  (Margaret Dianne), 1943- . Aussie Angels ; 6).

A823.3

Text design and typesetting by Bookhouse Digital, Sydney
Printed in Australia by Griffin Press, Adelaide

To my friend, Duane.
Love, Margaret

One

'What on earth's that noise?' said Mum.

The Green family were having breakfast on the veranda.

'It's Alice crunching toast,' said Mark.

Mike gave Alice a nudge with his foot to convey the message, 'Chew quietly or you'll be chucked out' and smiled across at Meg, who'd done the same thing.

Being twins, they often thought the same things and did the same things at exactly the same time.

'And it's *your* toast I can hear her crunching,' said Mum, looking sternly at Mark.

He had a habit of tossing his crusts under the table when he knew that Alice was lurking ready to gobble them up. She had the typical labrador's nature: she loved food.

'I can hear it now,' said Dad.

'What, Alice eating toast?' Mike nudged Alice again.

'No. It sounds like someone having a conversation in the garden.'

'Oh, I thought it was Mike's radio floating out through his window,' said Meg.

'I didn't turn it on this morning.'

Dad frowned. 'What the heck's going on?' He got to his feet and walked to the edge of the veranda. 'Who's there?'

'Mind your own business,' answered a cranky voice.

'This is private property and you can't stay here, whoever you are, so clear out,' Dad snapped angrily, as he walked down the steps.

'Ah, shut ya gob,' said the voice. It was

coming from the flowering gums and shrubbery near the side gate.

'What did you say?' Dad growled. 'You just come out here where I can see you, and—'

'Suck ya socks.'

'Now wait a minute—' Dad was getting really mad. He started walking towards the shrubbery.

'Be careful, dear,' called Mum.

'Alice isn't growling and barking like she usually does. In fact she's still chewing toast and couldn't care less. What's going on?' said Meg, frowning.

'It must be someone we know playing a joke,' answered Mike. 'We'd better go with Dad and check it out.'

They all followed behind Dad as he headed towards the gum trees.

'Come out of there *now*,' he said, with his hands on his hips, as Mum, the twins and Mark all bunched up behind him. 'This isn't funny!'

'Scratch ya bum. Go jump under a bus.'

With a whirr of wings a big white sulphur crested cockatoo flew out from the flowering gum and swooped off, cawing and squawking the way cockies do when they've been annoyed. It landed in a tall gum tree further up the driveway.

'Well, I'll be darned,' said Dad. 'A talking cocky. I wonder where that came from! It's obviously someone's pet. It must be lost.'

'I'd love a talking cocky, specially one that says heaps of cool stuff,' said Mark eagerly. 'Can we keep it, Dad?'

'No you can't. I'm not having a cocky that's been taught to say rude and cheeky things living here,' snapped Mum. 'I'd wash its mouth out with soap, that's what I'd do.'

Meg and Mike grinned at each other. That was an old remedy for "talking dirty" that Gran had threatened Mum with when she was a little girl. As far as they knew, Gran had never actually washed Mum's mouth out with soap, and Mum had never once done it to them if they dropped the occasional rude word. Mum merely raised her eyebrows and shook her head!

'Ya stink like dead squid ink,' yelled the cocky from the safety of its tree. 'Eat my shorts.'

'You haven't got any,' yelled Mark, dancing up and down.

'Suck snails,' called the cocky.

It took off, circled round them, and headed off towards the bush.

'Come back!' yelled Mark, running down the driveway after it. 'I'll give you some sunflower seeds.'

'Eat my shorts,' came floating through the air. 'Put a sock in it. Suck snails. Drop dead. Over and out.'

Everyone started laughing. Meg thought Mark was going to wet his pants he was laughing so much.

'We shouldn't be laughing. We're only encouraging him, if he's watching us,' said Mum, trying to look severe and failing miserably.

'Suck snails? Where'd it get that one from?' chuckled Dad, wiping his eyes. 'That bird's a real character, and I'll bet he belongs to a real character too. I didn't know a sulphur crested cockatoo could have such a wide vocabulary.'

The Greens returned to their breakfast, all except Mark.

'I've gotta go,' he said.

'Where?'

'To find the cocky.'

'But—'

It was too late. Mark had dashed through the house and they heard the front door slam as he went to get his bike. Only a few minutes later he came through the side gate and was pedalling fast down the driveway.

'I wanna find that cocky,' he yelled over his shoulder. 'Finders keepers.'

'In that case I hope he *doesn't* find it,' said Dad with a wry grimace. 'I don't need anyone else giving me a hard time round here.'

'Go with Mark, Alice,' said Mum firmly, and she gave the dog a nudge with her foot.

Alice abandoned the last crumbs and went to do her duty. She was tired of people nudging her with their feet. They'd been doing it all morning. Why couldn't they leave her to enjoy her toast in peace?

But Mark was such a little devil that anything could happen to him if she didn't keep a doggy eye out for trouble. So she went bounding down the driveway after him, woofing loudly.

'Get lost, Alice. Go back!'

Alice kept running and barked even louder.

'Shut that barking up,' called Mark over his shoulder. 'You're only going to scare the cocky.'

He'd known that Mum would send Alice after him. But he wanted to find the cocky, and a bounding, barking dog wasn't going to help the situation. Maybe if he rode faster he could leave her behind. He pushed even harder on the pedals.

Alice sighed. She didn't want to over-exert herself but there was no choice. She went into turbo mode and caught up to him, running alongside with her pink tongue hanging out.

'Woof,' she said.

'All right, all right, you can come, but… what did that cocky say? Put a sock in it, will you, Alice?'

Of course Mark had no idea where the cocky had gone. He'd grabbed some biscuits, as well as a big handful of sunflower seeds, and shoved them in his pocket. He was antic-ipating that he would hear the cocky screeching and could follow the sound. Then he figured that if he put the biscuits and the sunflower seeds on the ground and waited, the cocky would fly down to eat them. Then, with any luck, it would follow him home to get some more tasty snacks.

'Woof, woof,' said Alice, and went bound-ing off after a rabbit she'd spotted zooming into the undergrowth.

Mark slammed on the brakes.

'Alice,' he roared. 'Come here! *Now!* If you're gunna guard me, then make sure that you do a good job. You could get bitten by a snake or something, because it's spring and they're out of their winter holes and real cranky. And we haven't got time for you to get a snakebite if we're on a mission to find that cocky!'

Alice came back with her tail between her legs and looked apologetically up at Mark as if to say, 'Sorry. I got a bit distracted.'

It really was a beautiful spring day. The sky was the brightest blue, with just a few puffballs of cloud drifting lazily overhead. The birds were all singing and chirping, the bees were busy enjoying the sunshine. The gum trees smelt fresh and clean, and the air was heavy with the sent of bush myrtle and tea-tree blossom.

'Where *is* that cocky?' Mark put his head to one side and listened. Away in the distance he heard a loud, harsh screech.

'That's him!'

Mark went to pedal off and Alice grabbed him by the leg of his tracksuit pants.

'What are you doing, you stupid dog?'

'Grrr.' Alice didn't like being called stupid when she was only doing her job.

Mark knew that he wasn't allowed to go deeper into the forest by himself, even if she was with him.

Dad and Mum had rules. They weren't allowed to go further than the Old Mill Road on their own. That was one of the boundaries. They could go as far as the point on the beach and no further, or to the base of the big hill behind Animal Haven on the other side. And if Mark and Meg did have to go together on a mission and Mark was with them, they always had a rucksack with first aid equipment and a mobile phone.

Alice tugged harder.

'Let go, Alice,' sighed Mark. 'I know I have to go back. Maybe if I put a little pile of seeds here in this open space and then I make a trail that leads to Animal Haven, the cocky will find them and follow me. Maybe . . .'

Just then there was the most terrible raucous

screeching. It sounded like every bird in the whole forest was upset and yelling.

The kookaburras were cackling their heads off, the other cockies and galahs were screaming at their highest pitch, the magpies were carolling their lungs out and even the willy wagtail near Mark was bouncing up and down on a branch with its long black feathered tail quivering indignantly.

'Something's wrong,' cried Mark. 'Let go, Alice. We have to sort this out.'

With a jerk, Mark tugged at his tracksuit pants.

Rrrip went the material, and left a chunk in Alice's mouth.

Mark didn't care. All he knew was that there was big trouble in the Benwerrin forest, and he had to find out what! And it probably involved that cocky!

He took off up the Old Mill Road, standing hard on the pedals so he could get up the first hill.

Alice sighed, dropped the bit of his trakky

daks that she was still holding, and raced after him.

She knew that it was her duty to stay with Mark. But why hadn't the Greens given her an easier job?

Two

Mike and Meg were doing their chores when they heard the commotion.

'What on earth's that?' said Meg.

Carol the camel raised her haughty head and sniffed the air. It wasn't a bushfire because there was no smell of smoke.

And it couldn't be an earthquake because there were very few tremors at the lowest end of the scale in this part of the world. She knew that because she watched the Greens' TV through the loungeroom window.

And it wasn't a flood because it hadn't been raining. And it definitely wasn't a hurricane because there wasn't any wind to speak of.

No fire, earthquake, flood or hurricane. So what was the problem?

Whatever was disturbing the peace and quiet was making her nervous, even though it appeared to be far away and deep in the forest. Carol snorted and flared her nostrils. What was going on?

Elsie the emu cocked her head. There seemed to be a lot of her feathered friends making a heck of a hullabaloo in the distance. But as she didn't have any wings she couldn't very well fly away into the forest and see what was going on. So she went back to her job of pecking round for worms and bugs.

Cinnamon the koala, high up in her favourite tree, blinked her beady little eyes and waved a paw in the air crossly. Those stupid birds were making such a racket that even *she* couldn't sleep, despite having a tummy stuffed full of tasty gum leaves from her foraging the night before with her big male koala friend that the humans called Boss. She looked across at him. He was snoring away contentedly, curled into the fork of his own tree. It would take an atom bomb to disturb Boss!

The king parrots and rosellas who were in the aviary recovering from injuries flapped about agitatedly. Big Red started squawking in sympathy for his friends out in the forest.

Edna the echidna wasn't too fussed because she had her rear end up and head down, busily poking round for ants, but even her quills gave a little shiver and quiver when she heard the noise.

The only ones who weren't concerned were the nocturnal animals who were fast asleep in their dreys, logs, perches or pouches—Fur Bag the possum, Oscar the owl, and an assortment of babies.

Suddenly there was the sharp retort of a rifle in the distance. Shooting was illegal in the Otway Ranges because it was a national park.

'I reckon it's hunters. Or poachers,' said Dad angrily.

He'd been forking fresh hay into the stalls. Dropping the pitchfork he hurried outside, shading his eyes with his hand as he peered towards the mountains.

'I can't see anything.' Mike was beside Dad.

'Me neither.'

The squawking birds were now silent.

'It came from the Grey River reserve area. I'd better get my gun.'

In his position as the forest ranger Dad was legally entitled to carry a rifle, because sometimes, unfortunately, he had to put down an animal in agony if Uncle Pete couldn't get there in time. Of course he wasn't allowed to shoot humans who were causing trouble, but if they'd left a trail of dead animals behind them, which the illegal hunters sometimes did, he said he wished he *could* give them a taste of their own medicine and show them how agonising it would be to have a leg shot off or a bullet lodged in your body.

Professional hunters who had permits (although of course they couldn't shoot animals in State forests, unless it was a very special circumstance) always made sure they didn't leave any animals to suffer in agony.

Dad said that the hunters who went into the Otways to shoot were total *idiots* who had no respect for law and order, and who left behind them half-dead animals who then had to be put out of their misery by *him*.

Another problem in the forest was poachers who were after animals and birds to export illegally overseas. There was big money in selling parrots and cockatoos as pets, and now there were people in some countries who wanted their own pet kangaroo or koala or possum.

Meg and Mike thought that was just awful, because these animals were really native to Australia, and were happiest in the forest among the gum trees and not in someone's backyard or a cage in someone's living room.

'Where's Mark?' said Mum, as Dad was

about to jump in the patrol wagon. 'He shouldn't be wandering around on his own if there are poachers about.'

Dad bit his lip and frowned. 'He knows he's not allowed to cross the Old Mill Road,' he said. Then he looked at Meg and Mike. 'I think I'd better bring you two with me. If we find Mark you can ride back with him and make sure he gets here safely. Go and get your bikes and put them in the wagon.'

'Have you got your rucksacks ready?' asked Mum. 'And where are your mobiles?'

It was an unnecessary question really, because the rucksacks were always ready and the mobiles were kept charged up.

Just as Meg and Mike were lifting their bikes into the patrol wagon, they noticed a puff of dust approaching along the side road. Mike poked Meg in the ribs and grinned.

'Betcha I know what that is.'

'So do I.' She grinned back.

As the puff got closer they could see that it was actually Boris Boola going flat out on his old and trusty bike. He was coming to do his chores and take Carol for her exercise on the sandy beach nearby.

He skidded to a wild halt beside the patrol van.

'Don't ask: the answer's yes,' said Dad briskly. 'Toss your bike in. Hurry up. Let's go!'

Boris knew better than to ask where they were going. As a fully affiliated Aussie Angel he knew that Dad could be tense and terse when there was a job to do and he didn't appreciate a whole pile of questions. If you were an Angel you did as you were told and cooperated fully with whichever adult was in charge, otherwise you couldn't be one. There was no time to be spent rescuing a solitary Angel who'd decided to act like a careless daredevil and do his or her own thing. It always had to be a team effort.

'In the front, Boris,' said Dad when he went to clamber in beside Meg.

Mike winked at him. The Angels took turns to be the one who sat in the front beside Dad, because that person might have to operate the two-way radio when the mobile phone didn't work. Because Benwerrin Park was right on the edge of the Otway Ranges, sometimes signals couldn't travel over the mountains because they bounced back. There were quite a few places in the valleys which were what Dad called dead spots.

This was Boris's second turn in the front and he swelled with pride as he took his seat next to Dad. It showed that he, Boris Boola, ex loser, was trusted by the ranger one hundred per cent. And Boris knew that if Dad asked him to walk over hot coals with bare feet, dive into a shark-infested ocean or climb the highest mountain naked, he'd do it willingly.

Of course in reality Dad wouldn't ask him to do anything so weird or dangerous, but he might ask him to relay a message on the radio.

'I wonder which way Mark went?' mused Dad, as the wagon bumped along the track that led to Old Mill Road. 'If he's gone beyond the boundary...'

He left the rest of the sentence unfinished.

The punishment for going beyond the boundary and putting yourself in danger was a serious week's grounding, minimum! And no TV either.

Dad came to the crossroads and slowed down. 'Do I go up Old Mill Road looking for Mark or do I do up the Grey River road and find out what's going on?'

'Old Mill Road's pretty bumpy after the winter,' Mike offered. He was worried about Mark but also feeling he'd like to give his little brother a good talking to. Life at Animal Haven was busy enough without Mark causing an upset.

'He mightn't have come this way at all,' said Meg. 'He might have ridden down Hunt's Track or along the Kennet Track. There's just so many places he might have gone.'

'Well, can anyone see any sign that Mark's

been here? Or Alice?' Dad sounded impatient. 'A tyre mark? A paw print?'

'No. Wait!' Boris wound down his window and pointed. 'Is that a bit of his red trakky daks lying there?'

He opened the door, jumped out and picked it up. He brought it over to the van.

'Looks like it, all right,' said Meg, peering at the scrap of material.

'Looks like Mark's come this way then,' said Mike.

'And looks like I'm going to kill that kid when I find him. And that dog,' growled Dad. 'What the hell does he think he's doing, wandering round in the bush when it's a warm day and there's snakes popping out all over the place? I've got a job to do. I'm supposed to be protecting the animals and birds, not going on some wild goose chase after your brother!'

Everyone was quiet. Dad didn't lose his temper very often, which showed that he was really worried about Mark.

Then he sighed. 'Okay, I'll drive up Old Mill

Road, down Sabine Road and back round the Grey River road. In that way, even though it's slower, I hope we can find Mark and also find out what's going on in the forest and who's giving me grief.'

'What if Mark's taken a short cut along the wallaby track, down the fire break and gone home?' asked Boris.

'Then he'll be grounded *for the rest of his life* when I get my hands on him!' Dad snapped as he shoved the patrol van into four-wheel-drive. 'The only good thing about all this is that he's got Alice with him. If he gets lost she'll find the way home and drag him with her. Thank God we've got a labrador and not a chihuahua.'

Old Mill Road had been churned up by logging trucks and their tyres had made big ruts right along it. And the winter rains, roaring down the mountain, had made them worse. The patrol van bounced and bumped along the steep winding road.

There was no sign of Mark.

'That kid must've taken a short cut,' gritted

Dad. 'I just hope he doesn't meet an angry tiger snake. I just hope—'

They rounded a bend.

'There he is!' screamed Meg, leaning into the front seat and nearly stabbing Boris in the ear with her pointing finger.

'I know, I *know*. We've all got eyes,' said Dad tersely.

'I can't watch,' Mike muttered. 'Dad's gunna murder him.'

The patrol wagon pulled up alongside Mark.

'Get in!'

'Dad, I—'

'Just put your bike in the back and get in this van *now*!'

Alice put her tail between her legs and hung her head. She'd done her best to stop Mark but it hadn't been good enough. She gave an unhappy whine.

'It's okay, Alice,' said Dad. 'I know you did what you could. You've been hauling Mark out of trouble by the seat of his pants since the day he was born. You were a good dog to stay with him and not race off chasing rabbits or something.'

Alice hung her head even further. If Mark hadn't called her back she would still have been chasing that rabbit!

Mark and Alice scrambled into the wagon among the bikes and first aid gear.

'I hope we don't find an injured grey kangaroo or three or we'll have to tie them to the roof rack,' said Dad angrily. 'I'm going to turn round at the junction and you can all ride your bikes home. But Alice can stay with me because she looks worn out.'

Alice immediately tried to look even more pathetic. But secretly she was bursting with joy.

This was good news. The Aussie Angels and Mark had to ride their bikes back to Animal Haven while she got to sit in the van. And she loved it, because she could look out the window and watch for rabbits, roos and anything else that hopped, crawled or flew.

They reached the road junction in record

time and Dad kept the engine running while they unloaded the bikes.

'Right. You go straight home, do you hear me? I don't care if a spaceship lands in the middle of Old Mill Road and some alien jumps out and asks for directions, you're to stop for nothing and speak to no one till you get home. Got it?'

'Yes, Dad.'

'Yes, Mr Green.'

With a spurt of gravel from his tyres, Dad took off, with Alice hanging her head out the rear window and smiling happily.

'What made you do such a stupid thing?' said Mike angrily. 'We were on a mission, checking out that gun shot, and then we had to rescue you. And now we've got to take you home. You've spoilt our entire morning!'

Mark looked at Meg.

'He's right,' she said stiffly.

He looked at Boris, who stared straight ahead and didn't say a thing. As far as he was concerned this was a family matter, and although he was an Aussie Angel, he had to be careful because he didn't actually belong to the Green family.

'It's not fair,' said Mark, as the others took off down the hill on their bikes. 'You won't even *listen* to me. You won't give me a chance to explain. *It's just not fair!*'

Three

The Angels continued thumping and bumping on their bikes down Old Mill Road.

Mark was in front now with Mike, because he'd bleated, 'Wait for me' so much that the others got tired of it. Meg said he'd sounded like a cow having a calf, so to shut him up, they were letting him ride next to Mike. Also if the little devil was up the front they could all keep an eye on him.

Meg and Boris were riding behind. It was rough and tough going. Although there hadn't been any rain for a week the huge gums shaded the road and there were still slippery patches, not like at Animal Haven where the gravel road, unshadowed by trees, was dry and dusty.

'Eeeow!'

Meg did a massive skid, went into a three hundred and sixty degree spin-out, got totally out of control, and as her bike slewed sideways, she crunched into the trunk of a huge tree.

'Are you all right?' called Boris, slamming on his brakes and doing a controlled skid across the road.

'Hey. Wait!' he yelled after Mike and Mark. 'Meg's come off her bike.'

He knelt down beside her. The bike wheels were still spinning round madly, and Meg was lying there with her eyes shut. Then suddenly she opened them, blinked a few times, and sat up.

'I'm okay, just winded,' said Meg, grinning at him. 'It takes more than an old gum tree to stop me.'

'Just as well you were wearing your stackie,' said Boris gruffly. 'You could've killed yourself.'

He was fond of Meg; in fact, he thought she was wonderful. For a girl. He didn't have any sisters so he didn't know much about the female species except that the ones in school seemed to giggle and gossip all the time. Meg was more like a good mate.

She stood up and wiped the mud and leaves off her jeans, and was picking up her bike as the others came back.

'What happened?' asked Mike.

'You should've seen the donut she did,' said Boris. 'What a beauty.'

'We haven't got time to be doing donuts and wheelies,' snapped Mike. 'We're supposed to be getting home in a hurry.'

'The skid was accidental,' Boris cut in. 'She didn't *mean* to do it!' He put his hands on his hips and glared at Mike. 'She could've killed herself!'

'Oh.' Mike immediately looked contrite. 'Sorry, Sis.'

'Can we hurry up?' said Mark petulantly. 'I've got things to do!'

Coming from Mark that was a bit much, seeing he'd caused all the hassles in the first place.

'Yeah. Move it an' groove it,' said this raucous voice. 'Pull ya socks up. On ya bike.'

'It's my cocky!' yelled Mark, dumping his bike carelessly on the ground and jumping about like he had prickles in his pants. 'I can hear him. But I can't see him. Where is he?'

'Everybody out. Everybody out. She's gunna blow,' squawked the cocky.

The Angels looked at each other and started to laugh.

'What's gunna blow?' yelled Boris at the cocky, who was dancing along a broad branch and bobbing its head up and down.

'Blow ya brains out,' said the cocky. 'Over and out.'

Mark was so excited. Here was the lost cocky, just above his head. He shoved his hand

in his pocket and pulled out some broken biscuits and a handful of sunflower seeds.

'Cocky wanna cracker?' he called hopefully,
holding out his hand.

'No, Cocky wants a Tim Tam,' said the
cocky, and with a swoosh he flew down from
the tree and landed on Mark's shoulder.

Then he marched down Mark's arm and
looked at the food with his head cocked on
one side. Deliberately he pecked out the bis-
cuit pieces and spat them on the ground. He
cracked the sunflower seeds in his strong beak
and—*pfft*—spat out the husks.

'Hey, he's heavy,' said Mark, using his other
arm as a prop. 'He weighs a tonne.'

'Heavy Eddy,' said the cocky with his head
on one side again. He looked at Mark with his
bright shrewd eyes. 'Heavy Eddy.'

'Maybe that's his name. Heavy Eddy.'

'More than likely he's just Eddy,' said Boris,
stroking the cocky with a cautious finger.

That strong beak could inflict a nasty nip
if Eddy decided to be unfriendly.

'Eddy. *Eddy*,' said the cocky, looking at Boris very seriously.

'No I'm *Boris*. Are you Eddy?'

'Ready Eddy. Ready to rock 'n' roll,' answered the cocky, bobbing his head so that his yellow crest waved like a banner.

The Angels knew that this crest was actually a kind of flag to signal the bird's state of arousal or alarm. It could be raised or lowered to reveal or conceal a fan of bright yellow feathers. The flash of colour acted as a warning to other birds, because cockies were bossy and liked to rule the forest. The Angels also knew that the cockatoo family were the only birds who could raise and lower their crests.

But like the other parrots, they had a strong foot with two toes pointing forward and two back, so they could pick up food and put it in their beaks. And they did this nearly all day long!

'Oh, he's lovely. I want to keep him forever,' said Mark, stroking the gleaming white feathers.

'Kiss Cocky. Kiss Cocky,' said Eddy, and rubbed his beak gently against Mark's cheek.

He was really beautiful.

'Right,' said Mark. 'That's *it*. I love you, you love me, you're mine, and you're coming home with me. Hand me my bike please, Meg.'

Meg was smiling as she picked up Mark's bike.

'Hop on the handlebar, Eddy,' said Mark. 'We're going for a ride.'

'On ya bike,' squawked Eddy happily. 'On ya bike. Rack off. Over and out.'

The Angels, Mark and the cocky too went bumping down the hill. The cocky loved Mark's bike. It leaned forward with the wind whistling through its crest, hung on with its strong claws and made little clucking noises.

Mark was riding carefully because he didn't want to hurt his new friend. Of course he'd forgotten that if anything unexpected happened, the cocky would fly safely into a tree.

'Wait till Carol meets Eddy,' he said, as they

came to the junction of Old Mill Road and the home track. 'She'll love my cocky too.'

Boris rolled his eyes heavenwards but didn't say a thing. He couldn't see what a camel and a cocky would have in common.

Once they hit the flat stretch, Mark went boring along the road towards home, his legs going so fast that the others could hardly see his feet.

He went roaring up the driveway and yelled at the top of his lungs, 'Mum! *Mum!* I found the cocky!'

'Get a life! Get a life!' screeched Eddy as Mum came running onto the veranda to see what all the fuss was about.

'I found the cocky!' He screamed to a halt as Eddy gripped the handlebars tighter so he didn't go careering off into space.

'Actually, Eddy found *us*,' grinned Meg, skidding up alongside Mark.

'Meg. Look at your jeans. What on earth have you been doing? Rolling in the mud?'

'She fell off her bike,' said Mark, 'but don't

worry about *her*. Look at *my cocky*! He says his name's Eddy.'

'Steady Eddy,' said the cocky, falling off the handlebars and playing dead on the lawn.

'That confounded cockatoo,' said Mum, trying to keep a straight face. 'I suppose you're going to want to keep it as a pet?'

'Give us a kiss,' said Eddy, opening one eye and looking at Mum. 'Give us a kiss. Over and out.'

'He really is a character,' she laughed. 'All right. He can stay. But we'll have to try and find his owner. Someone must've taught him all these sayings.'

'Your shout,' said Eddy. 'Your shout. Make it a double.'

'Maybe he just picked all this stuff up as he flew round the countryside,' said Mark, who didn't want to return Eddy to his rightful owner. 'I own him now.'

'Judging by his conversation, his owner's some old man who loves cigarettes and whisky and wild, wild women,' said Mum. 'And, speaking of wild women, where's Alice?'

'Dad found me on Old Mill Road and took Alice with him,' Mark explained.

'And of course you know that you're now grounded for a week for going beyond the boundary and causing a whole lot of trouble?'

Mark hung his head and tried to look mournful, but right now he didn't care if he was grounded for a year. He had a talking cocky, all of his own and he could keep it in his bedroom. It could sit on his bedhead and eat Tim Tams, and he could teach it cool stuff, like "Mark's a legend" and "Kara Bronley's a loser".

He had his special friend Selina the seal, but she couldn't exactly sit on the bedhead, could she? Selina lived on the rocky point with the big old bull seal called Samuel—that is, when she wasn't swimming in the sea.

Yes, thought Mark, as Mum kept rabbiting on about how naughty he'd been. A talking cocky would be so cool!

Four

'Okay. There's been enough time wasted,' said Mum. 'We've got the baby animals to feed. Your dad phoned to say he's heading towards the Number 3 track at the back of Mount Sabine because he suspects that's where the disturbance is. I'm not too happy about him being out there on his own when there's someone roaming round with a rifle, so if he's not back in an hour I'm going to get Uncle Pete and look for him. So put your bikes away and start your chores, please.'

'Okay, Mum,' said Mike.

'You too, Mark.'

'Can my cocky come too?'

'So long as he doesn't upset the animals or cause any mischief,' said Mum, wagging her finger sternly at Eddy.

'Suck ya toenails,' said the cheeky cocky, then, seeing the look on Mum's face, he bobbed his head up and down. 'You're gorgeous. Give us a kiss.'

'Er, come on, Eddy,' said Mark hurriedly, picking up his new feathered friend and balancing him on the bike's handlebars, before he changed from compliments back to insults.

But Eddy immediately scrambled onto Mark's shoulder and sat there looking defiant.

'Hurry up, Mark,' said Boris, holding the side gate open. 'I've got too much work to do to be hanging around waiting for you.'

'Bag ya head,' said Eddy.

'I wonder if that cocky knows anything nice and polite?' Meg glared at Eddy.

'You're gorgeous. Over and out!'

'He can certainly turn on the charm when he wants to,' said Boris drily, as they went round the back of the house to start their chores.

Carol the camel bellowed in delight when she saw Boris, and she left her spot at the window where she'd been watching U2 on 'TV's *Latest Video Hits*', because in all the hullabaloo Mum had forgotten to turn the set off. She came lolloping over to him, but she stopped short when she noticed Eddy on Mark's shoulder.

'Carol, this is Eddy. Eddy, this is Carol,' said Mark.

'Hrumph,' said Carol, looking the cocky up and down.

'You're gorgeous. Gorgeous. Give us a kiss. Over and out,' said Eddy.

Carol bared her yellow teeth in a sickly smile and gently blew her camel breath onto Eddy, ruffling his feathers.

Eddy politely decided not to say anything about her bad breath and raised his crest up and down to show that he was pleased but a bit wary. He'd never seen a camel before and he wasn't quite sure whether she ate cockatoos or not.

'I'd better introduce you to everyone,' said Mark to his cocky. 'That's Elsie the emu.'

Eddy knew about emus. He thought they were stupid. Why didn't they flap their wings and take off when there was danger, instead of running like a jet-propelled feather duster along the ground?

'Look up there. See? That's Cinnamon and Boss the koalas.'

Eddy knew about koalas. He liked to tease them by flying above their heads and annoying them. They were such sluggish, slow-thinking creatures, always asleep or chewing gum leaves. He liked to give them a bit of a shake-up sometimes.

'This is Edna the echidna. And Grey Boy the roo,' added Mark. 'Lots of the animals are fast asleep, and I guess you mightn't ever get to meet them, because you'll be asleep when they're awake. Now there's Selina, but she lives at the beach, and—'

'Mark. Would you stop yabbering and *do some work*?' yelled Mike.

'Up ya nose with a rubber hose,' said Eddy.

'You with the feathers! Behave yourself or you'll be cockatoo stew!' said Mum, coming round the corner with a basketful of washing.

Eddy immediately flew off Mark's shoulder and landed on the clothesline. Gripping the wire with his beak, he started whirling round and round, over and over.

'Whoa. Look at him go!' shouted Mark.

'What?' called Mike from the shed. He came out to see what was happening. And Meg poked her head out of the surgery where she was scrubbing the floor.

Boris glanced up from weeding the garden. Carol peered over, too. What was going on?

When he knew he had everyone's attention, Eddy suddenly stopped whirling round and round. He sat up straight, then flew down and picked up a sock.

'Hey, bring that back!' roared Mum.

But Eddy flew back onto the clothesline, draped the sock over the wire, unclipped a peg with his beak, then snapped it firmly onto the sock!

'He's helping you to hang out the washing!' said Meg in amazement, as Eddy flew down again to get the other sock.

They'd all seen the king parrots attack the pegs with their beaks and swing on the clothesline, but they'd never seen a bird who could peg out the washing.

'He should be on TV,' said Boris.

At once Mark went rushing inside to get the video camera. He'd already won a prize for his filming of Elsie the emu getting tangled in the washing. Maybe this could go on *Harry's Practice* or *Today Tonight*.

Last week there'd been footage of a dog that could climb a ladder carrying tools in its mouth on request. A cocky that could hang out washing was far more impressive than that and Mark tore outside to start filming.

Eddy immediately started showing off in between all the pegging. He did a little dance along the wire. He put his crest up and down. He postured and he posed as he hung out Mike's undies, Dad's shirt, and Mum's T-shirt.

'You're not that smart,' said Mum. 'You've got that T-shirt bunched up in one corner.'

Eddy gave her a dirty look. He was only a bird after all. What was her problem?

'Say something, Eddy,' said Mark, zooming in for a close-up.

'Give us a kiss,' said Eddy, bowing. 'Dreamin'. Dreamin'. Suck ya socks. Jump under a bus. Rock 'n 'roll. Awk. Awk.'

Boris was rolling round on the lawn and clutching his sides, sore with laughter. Carol gave Eddy a nasty look. *She* was the one Boris was in love with, not *him*! Striding over to the clothesline, she stuck her head between him and the camera lens and smiled lovingly at Boris.

Eddy immediately flew onto her head and started bobbing up and down.

'Burger with the lot,' he squawked. 'Get a life. Bag ya head. Over and out!'

Carol tossed her head but Eddy hung on tighter.

Suddenly Elsie the emu started running round and round the backyard. She wasn't sure what was going on and she knew that she couldn't climb up onto the clothesline and do wheelies and whirlies, but she knew she could run in circles. If that was what it took to get on *Australia's Funniest Home Video* again, she'd do it.

'That emu's gone mad,' said Mike.

'She's gone mad,' screeched Eddy. 'Drop dead. Over and out!'

'I give up,' said Mum, collapsing on the grass. 'This is better than a circus!'

'I certainly hope that an owner doesn't come forward when we advertise that we've found him,' whispered Meg, 'because it will break Mark's heart.'

'Yeah.' Mike chewed his lip and looked worried. 'I've got a horrible feeling that this cocky's been trained by a professional or something. He's too clever by far to be someone's backyard pet. I reckon he's in Actors Equity too, because he's a real show-off and he loves acting.'

'Maybe that's how we can trace his owner.'

Mike looked at Mark and then at the cocky. They were so happy together.

'But the problem is—do we want to?'

Just then their neighbour Annie came strolling round the path with her sister, Gladys, who was staying with her for a few days.

'Hi,' said Mum. 'With all the commotion going on, we didn't hear your car.'

'Just calling to see if you want anything in town,' said Annie.

'That's nice of you, but—'

Suddenly in the distance there was the sound of a gun going off again.

Mum froze. 'That sounded like it came from the Mount Sabine area,' she said. 'It's got to mean trouble!'

Five

'Call Uncle Pete and get him to meet me at Number 3 track,' said Mum, as she rushed towards her station wagon. 'I *hope* that's where your father is, because that's where he said he was going. Although with someone shooting, I'm kind of hoping he isn't in the same area! I'm really worried. Why hasn't he contacted me by now?'

'He might've just shot a snake,' said Mark.

'Mum, I think we'd better come with you,'

said Mike. 'It could be dangerous for you to go tearing off into the forest by yourself.'

'Someone's got to mind the animals,' Boris pointed out, as Meg grabbed her mobile from her pocket and started dialling. 'And we can't drive, so we're the ones who have to stay here.'

'Do you want *us* to come with you?' Annie asked Mum. 'Or we can stay here and mind the animals for you if you like while you all go. We're quite happy not to drive to town, aren't we, Gladys?'

Her sister nodded. She loved the animals and was hoping they could stay and mind the refuge on their own. Then she could have a nice cuddle of the joeys.

'That's kind of you,' said Mum. 'Yes, I think—'

'Wait. Here's Alice!' yelled Mike.

The big labrador came pounding round the corner, her pink tongue hanging out and her sides heaving with the effort of having run for kilometres through the forest. Being a smart dog she'd taken a short cut, but it had been scary when she'd met a tiger snake poised to strike, and painful when she'd stepped on a bull ants' nest.

'What's wrong, girl? Where's Dad?' asked Mum, squatting down to talk to her.

'Woof, woof, woof,' yelped Alice, leaping about. She started whining and pawing the ground, then ran towards the driveway, and barked loudly and urgently.

'Come here, Alice,' said Mum, and Alice came trotting back, trying to wag her tail but looking very anxious. 'You're trying hard to tell us something, aren't you? Okay, settle down. Boris, you talk to her,' said Mum, trying to stay calm.

Boris squatted beside Mum, concentrating hard on the thought pictures he was receiving from Alice. He had this special gift of being able to talk with animals by interpreting their thought pictures (because animals didn't think in words like humans) so he was the logical one to find out what had happened.

'Hmm,' he said to Alice, pursing his lips. 'Okay, girl. You're doing your best.'

'What?' Mum interrupted, grasping his sleeve urgently. 'What's she telling you?'

'Well, it's a bit jumbled because she's got about twenty thought pictures all going on at once, but as near as I can gather, Mr Green's found something suspicious. I think it's a car. So he left his van to investigate, then it gets all blurry.'

'He should have phoned,' said Mum.

'Maybe he tried to and couldn't get through. Or maybe he didn't have time. It's a bit fuzzy. I'm trying to work out—What, girl?'

Boris concentrated as Alice yelped and barked and pawed at the ground. 'Calm down. I can't understand what you're trying to tell me if you start to panic.'

'Put a sock in it,' squawked Eddy. 'Drop dead. Over and out!'

'I tell you, I'll strangle that cocky in a minute,' said Mum.

Mark quickly grabbed Eddy and moved away from Alice, Mum, Boris and the visitors.

'This is serious stuff,' he said to Eddy. 'It's not time to be making smart remarks. *Keep quiet*.'

'Put up or shut up,' said Eddy.

'Exactly!'

Alice had calmed down. She was now gazing steadily at Boris as he tried to translate her thoughts.

'I think she's saying that the patrol van had a crash or something,' he said, looking worried. 'I can't make it out properly. There's something about a gun. No, it's all fuzzy.'

'Oh, no,' moaned Mum.

'Hang on. I think Mr Green's—,' Boris frowned. 'I don't get this bit. He's sort of disappeared. Maybe he's inside the van. I just don't know.'

'What do you mean?'

'It's too confusing so I don't know.'

'I can't get Uncle Pete: only his answering service, so I left a message for him to meet you at the Number 3 Track, seeing as that's where Dad was going,' said Meg, getting off the phone. 'I think we'd better come with you because we don't know what's going on and you shouldn't be out there on your own. It could take ages for Uncle Pete to get there.'

'I could stay here with Mark,' said Boris.

'We might need you to talk to Alice,' said Mum. 'Meg's right. If there's injured people, birds or animals, we're going to need all the help we can get. Let's go.'

Everyone but Annie and Gladys piled into Mum's station wagon. She'd only had it for two weeks. It had a bull bar at the front and was a four-wheel-drive as well, so it could bush-bash through the scrub and handle the ruts on Number 3 track.

'We'll stay here till you get back,' called Annie, as Mum revved the engine. 'Animal Haven's in safe hands, so don't worry. I hope you find that everything's okay. Bye.'

'Annie's such a good neighbour and friend,' said Mum, whipping down the driveway and turning left towards the Grey River road. 'I don't know what I'd do without her.'

Meg was in the front with Mum, and the boys and Alice were in the back. Mum reached the junction of the Great Ocean Road and the Grey River road just as a log truck came hurtling round the corner, going too fast. It missed them by centimetres.

'Learn to drive, ya mug!' screeched Eddy out the window. 'Drop dead. Over and out.'

'Oh, no!' Mum glared in the rear vision mirror. 'I thought Mark was staying behind with Annie. I didn't realise he was with us. This could be dangerous. And what's that bird doing here? I didn't say you could come along and bring that cocky too.'

'And you didn't say I couldn't,' said Mark jauntily.

'Don't be cheeky!'

'I got that truck's number,' said Meg. 'We should report him, Mum. He could kill some-one, going that fast round the Great Ocean Road. There's all these tourists driving along at about twenty five k, and if he came screaming round a bend, they wouldn't have a hope.'

'The trucks shouldn't even be on this road,' added Mike. 'I thought they had to take the road to Colac.'

'There's always someone who doesn't obey the rules,' said Mum, as she accelerated up the Grey River road and past the snoozing koala colony who lived in the trees past the first bend.

'Eddy rules,' said Eddy cheerfully. 'Eat dirt and die.'

But Mum couldn't help smiling as the others stifled their giggles.

'That cocky's incorrigible,' she said.

'What's that mean?' asked Boris.

'Incurably naughty,' said Mum.

'Drop dead,' said Eddy. 'Suck snails. Put a sock in it. Over and out!'

'*You'll* be out in a minute if you don't shut up,' said Mum. 'Out the window on a one-way flight in the opposite direction. So if I were you, *I'd put a sock in it*.'

'Yer a hard woman,' muttered Eddy as Mum drove over the Grey River bridge. 'Yer a hard woman. Keep yer shirt on. Over and out.'

'Try Dad's mobile now.' Mum ignored the cocky and spoke tersely to Meg, who began dialling immediately.

'Nothing,' said Meg after a few seconds. 'It just says this mobile is unavailable and to leave a message.'

Mum looked grim as she swung the wheel and headed the station wagon off the road and onto the Number 3 track. She was beginning to think she'd been too hasty in bringing the children with her, even though the Angels were better at surviving in the bush and finding their way round in the forest than she was herself. Even Mark was a good little bushman, except that he was too impetuous and didn't always stick to the rules.

But right now they didn't know what they were going to find along this track that led deeper into the forest.

Or *who*!

Six

As the wagon bounced along the track, mud from the puddles splashed all over the windscreen.

Just as on Old Mill Road, the sun didn't shine through the thick canopy of tree ferns and gums along parts of this track, so even though it hadn't rained for nearly a week, the surface was boggy and slippery. Number 3 track was a dry-weather-only narrow trail through the bush, mainly for use by firefighters in the summer bushfire season.

There were quite a lot of tracks like this throughout the Otway Ranges. Sometimes people with four-wheel-drives went for treks, and camped in small clearings off to the side of the road.

And certain people grew marijuana illegally deep in the Ranges, using the tracks to go a long way into the forest before blazing their own trails even deeper. Every now and then the police would send in helicopters to try and find the crops, but it was hard because they were well hidden.

And sometimes poachers used the tracks for their own illegal operations, also blazing their own offshoot trails so they could set up their traps and catch unwary animals and birds.

One of the saddest things about this illegal trade was that often the birds were smuggled into other countries in packing cases with only a few air holes punched in the sides, and if these got blocked up during the journey, the birds would die. Meg and Mike thought the people doing this were the cruellest, meanest humans on earth, and when they heard that poachers were in the area, they were really angry.

Mum was a good driver, but it took a lot of concentration to cope with the tricky conditions on this track. She did a few skids but knew to let the wagon come naturally out of its slide. So she didn't wrench the steering wheel or put her foot hard on the brake.

'Look, there's where someone's got bogged,' cried Meg, pointing at the churned-up mud which Mum had skilfully avoided.

'Must've been the poachers,' said Mike. 'Dad wouldn't get bogged.'

Everyone knew that the edges were soft and spongy, and if a vehicle went off the slippery but firm track surface, the wheels would sink down into the mud.

'Whoever it was got out,' said Mark, craning his neck to see better.

'More's the pity,' said Mum grimly.

The wagon crawled up a steep hill. The

track was much drier now as the sun shone
strongly through the trees. Obviously there was
always more dampness at the foot of the mountains and they'd just come through quite a
deep valley, with steep inclines on either side.

Everyone breathed a sigh of relief. It was a
bit spooky in the dank and gloomy forest, but
up here the birds were chirping and the wattle
was bursting into bloom, making a beautiful
golden tunnel to drive through.

Suddenly Mum hit the brakes.

'What's wrong?'

'I think we've missed a sidetrail,' she said.
'No one's been along this part for quite a
while.'

'How do you know?' asked Mark from the
back.

'No broken twigs from a passing vehicle
brushing the sides, no scattered blossoms, and
a large fallen branch just ahead blocking the
road,' said Mum calmly, as she prepared to
reverse into a small clearing.

There was little chance of getting bogged

here, but just the same, Mum was careful to keep the wheels on the hard surface.

'You could be a detective,' said Boris, admiringly.

'She reads enough crime books.' Meg grinned sideways at her mother.

'Yeah. And that might come in handy,' said Mike quietly. 'I've got a bad feeling about all this.'

They were silent as Mum drove the wagon slowly back along the road. Their eyes were scanning the bush, looking for any clues, any signs of a vehicle leaving the main track.

'Eyes right,' squawked Eddy suddenly from his perch along the rear shelf. 'Eyes right. Over and out.'

'I can't see anything,' said Mum, braking gently. They opened the window and leaned out.

'Yes. *There!*'

Whoever it was had been shrewd all right. The wheel marks had been erased from the road with a branch and the lead-in to the side track cleverly camouflaged with several broken branches.

'Someone doesn't want us to follow this trail,' said Mike grimly, as Meg tried again to contact Uncle Pete on the mobile.

'I just can't get a connection,' she put it down again in exasperation.

'We've got a couple of flares in the rucksack,' said Mike. 'Do you reckon we should use them now, or wait till we find Dad?'

Mum frowned. 'We might need them later,' she said. 'We're not sure that your dad went along this trail till we follow it. But I'm worried about you children. I'm not acting like a responsible parent, leading you all into danger. What would your mother say, Boris, if she knew I was doing this?'

'She'd say, "Stop muckin' round and get on with it", that's what she'd say,' said Boris firmly, as he opened the rear door and got out of the car.

He started pulling the branches out of the way. Mike joined him while Meg walked along the main track and drew a big arrow on the slippery surface. Then she wrote, "Uncle Pete, this way!" in big writing.

Mark started putting twigs on the arrow to make it stand out more so that any motorist, Uncle Pete or not, would see it, even if it was night time.

Alice had a quiet and reflective pee near the base of a large tree. She'd already sniffed the scent of strange human beings and knew that they'd driven into the forest. But she had to wait for her family to do their stuff and then drive her further down the new trail before she could do *her* stuff!

With his head cocked to one side Eddy looked at the busy humans from his new perch on the roof rack.

The trouble with humans, even nice ones like this lot, was that they couldn't get a bird's eye view of things. And that dog might be friendly, but she was thick in the head if she thought that peeing near a tree was going to solve anything!

With a squawk, Eddy flew into the air. 'See ya later, alligator,' he called as he soared away into the trees.

'He's gone! Do something!' yelled Mark, jumping up and down. 'Come back, Eddy.'

'I think he's gone for a bit of an aerial reconnaissance,' said Boris.

'What's an air real cog sands?'

'An aerial reconnaissance means he's sussing out the situation from above,' explained Mike, and he winked at Boris, who was trying not to laugh and hurt Mark's feelings.

'Okay, kids, let's go,' said Mum, climbing back into the wagon. 'But if there's any danger, we're pulling out.'

'And if anyone starts shooting, lie on the floor,' advised Boris. 'I know about these things.'

No one was going to argue with Boris. After all, his own brother Brendan Boola had shot him when Boris was trying to protect Alice. The Boola boys were bad news, although at the moment two were in jail and three had cleared off interstate. Or that's where they were supposed to be.

Mum started the engine and the wagon rumbled slowly down the rough trail which then began to widen out and become quite smooth.

'Someone's even dumped loads of gravel along here,' said Mike in amazement. 'This trail's heaps better than Number 3!'

'It could have another exit,' said Boris. 'If I was a crook, I'd have three or four escape routes planned, a bit like a rabbit.'

'Or an echidna,' said Meg. 'Edna's got three holes in our backyard as well as her hollow log, and I'll bet they all lead to the same burrow.'

'A platypus does the same thing,' Mike added. 'But it's got two or three entrances to its burrow.'

'Come to think of it, so do we,' smiled Mum. 'A front door, a side door and a back door.'

'And windows,' blurted Mark. 'I often climb out my window and—ooops!'

He'd just given himself away.

The others all grinned at each other because they all knew how often he sneaked out that window, even if Mum didn't.

Alice barked. She knew a bit about windows too, but she knew heaps about holes and burrows. She was an *expert*. She'd spent hours tracking that echidna all over the yard with her nose. She knew exactly where Edna's central room was located—right under the pear tree next to the garden fence. In fact, just for fun, she'd started digging into it and got a spiked nose for her trouble. So now there was one thing Alice did know: it was that her nose and Edna's quills were not compatible!

'I reckon we'll come to some traffic lights soon,' said Mike, gazing out with interest as the tree ferns brushed against the car window. 'This road's so well made. Someone's had a lot of money to have done this. They would've needed a grader and trucks.'

'Traffic lights? But there's no electricity poles.' Mark stared at Mike in bewilderment.

'Just a joke, dumbat,' said Mike, ruffling his hair. 'I meant that this road is used by vehicles that don't get bogged in the bush, because someone's built them a nice road, even better than Number 3 track, so they *don't* get bogged.'

'Which means they're in a hurry to get in and out of here,' said Mum.

'It'd be hard to spot this road from a helicopter because the cliffs are so steep and the trees are so dense here.'

Meg was squinting up through the overhanging ferns and bushes.

'Maybe there's a secret army camp,' said Boris, frowning.

'I've never heard of a secret army camp in these parts,' said Mum.

'But then it wouldn't be a secret, would it?' he rejoined.

Secret army camp or not, the Aussie Angels didn't care, just as long as they found Dad safe and well.

Seven

The gravel road wound round the bottom of the hill, almost running parallel to a small creek which gurgled and tumbled over the smooth green rocks. Every now and then the road went further into the tall trees but would curve back again alongside the creek.

'Could be a speed operation,' said Boris.

'Speed? Why would someone want to cars out here?' asked Mum.

'No I mean *drug* speed, not *car* spe Boris. 'You see, they need a lot of make drugs called amphetamines, and a secret place as well, but usually it happens nearer to towns and cities, not in the middle of nowhere.'

'Why's it called speed?' asked Meg.

'Because it speeds people up. They think they can party all night and bop till they drop,' Boris explained. 'And some truck drivers use it to stay awake on long trips. But it can mess up their driving skills, so it's not good stuff.'

'Maybe that was what was wrong with the one who nearly ran into us before,' said Meg.

'He just took the corner too fast,' said Mum. 'I really think your imagination's running away with you, Boris. Secret army camps and now an amphetamine factory?'

Boris shrugged. 'It's another world out there, Mrs Green,' he said. 'You never know what crooks will do to make money, and speed's a good money spinner if you can get away with it.'

'I hope they're not putting this speed stuff n the creek then,' said Mark crossly. 'All the animals will be in turbo mode. Kangaroos leaping tall buildings and koalas swinging from trees like trapeze artists.'

Everyone started giggling at the thought of kangaroos leaping tall buildings in a single bound and koalas swinging from trees wearing spangled tights, not that there actually were any tall buildings and spangled tights in the Otways, but—

'I don't think—' began Mum as they rounded a bend and came to a crossroad with quite a large clearing beyond. There was a startled gasp.

Dad's patrol van was parked in the clearing.

And they couldn't see anyone!

Mum slammed on the brakes and everyone leapt out and raced over to it.

The van was empty.

'Dad,' shouted Mike, cupping his hands. *'Dad! Coo-ee! Coo-ee!'*

Mum was busy investigating the interior of the patrol van as Mark poked his head through the rear doors.

'There's blood,' he yelled. 'Dad's been shot!'

The others rushed to have a look.

'I think that's blood from the wallaby that he rescued the other day,' said Meg, inspecting the small fleck which had somehow escaped Mike's notice when he'd cleaned the van.

'Don't do that again, Mark,' said Mum crossly. 'You nearly gave me a heart attack!'

Mark looked crestfallen. It *could* have been Dad's blood! How was he to know it was only a wallaby's? He was only trying to be *helpful*.

He wandered off along the road, looking for signs of a struggle, anything that could show that Dad had been kidnapped. Or, ranger-napped.

Alice had her nose to the ground, sniffing for clues. Strangers had been here, talking to Dad. Five of them. All males. Three big ones and two smaller ones. She wrinkled her labrador face in concentration. Two of these smells she thought she recognised. And her nose could always be trusted. It never got a smell mixed up or confused.

It was her brain that sometimes got confused.

Like now. Where had she smelt those two humans before?

Trouble was, she couldn't follow Dad's scent or that of the men because apparently Dad had been bundled into a vehicle and driven off but it wasn't clear which direction they'd gone.

Meg and Boris peered at the ground, looking for evidence.

'There's been some sort of struggle over here,' called Meg. 'The grass is flattened and the edge of the road's been churned up. That's a man's footprint.'

'Is it Dad's?'

They all crouched to have a closer look.

'Large prints,' said Boris.

'Someone else had small feet with big ripples on the soles of his shoes,' said Mike, pointing. 'See?'

'Runners,' said Boris. 'Probably Nikes: look at the tread. Hmmm...'

He pressed his lips together and slammed

his fist into his palm as if he was wishing it was someone's chin.

'I know who wears runners like that,' he said slowly. 'And I know he's bad enough to be involved in something crook too.'

'Who? Not your brother?'

'Well, *all* of my brothers love to be involved in bad things, not just one of them, but I reckon this print belongs to Greash.'

'What?' The Angels stared at Boris with their mouths hanging open.

Mum frowned. 'Boris, you can't go round accusing boys that you don't like,' she said severely.

'Who else at school wears pump-ups with huge thick treads and would be roaming round in the bush?'

'Yeah,' said Mark. 'I reckon Greash and Foxie have kidnapped Dad! Call the cops. No, fire the flares.'

'Wait a minute,' Mum interrupted briskly. 'These small footprints could belong to *anyone*. First of all, this road actually comes from somewhere, maybe from Dean's Marsh for all we know. There could've been bushwalkers here, or campers, or anyone. It's no good suspecting your ex friend Greash, even though he is a bit on the wild side. That won't help find your father!'

Alice threw back her head and howled with frustration. There were no scents to follow. Where was Dad?

'It's okay, Alice,' whispered Meg. 'We'll find Dad. Don't worry.'

'Mum's right,' said Mike to Boris as they hurried back to the wagon. 'Greash and Foxie don't drive cars. They couldn't kidnap Dad on their bikes, could they!'

'Yeah, but Greash's dad is a real nasty guy and Foxie's step-dad's *evil*,' said Boris. 'I wouldn't put anything past those two. And their friends aren't so flash either. I reckon it's them helping some crooks. They've been throwing a bit of money round lately too. Greash and Foxie wanted me to rejoin the gang. They said they could show me how to earn heaps to pay for Carol's upkeep and I'd have plenty left over to have some fun.'

'What did you say?'

Meg had overheard the conversation and stopped short, horrified that Boris might be tempted to take up again with those two bullies and thugs.

'What did I say?' Boris looked her straight in the eye as they all piled into the wagon. 'I told them to get lost!'

'Get lost. Get lost,' squawked a familiar voice as Eddy flew down from a tree nearby.

'Eddy!' shrieked Mark gleefully. 'You came back to me.' He wound down the window. 'Get in!'

But Eddy decided to ride on the roof rack. He got a much better view from up there, plus he didn't have smelly dog breath in his face all the time. Didn't that dog know it needed its teeth cleaned or a good mouth wash?

'Hey. He came back,' breathed Mark happily, craning his neck out the window and getting his face swiped by a stray tree fern frond.

'Like a boomerang,' said Mum drily, although her hands were trembling as she turned the key in the ignition and started driving down the right hand fork of the road, which soon began to narrow into a bumpy track. Her nerves were beginning to get frayed and she was desperately worried about her husband and what was going on.

'It's okay, Mum. We'll find Dad.' Meg reached across and patted her hand. 'But is this the right way?' Mum looked so tired.

Mark stuck his head out the window again. 'Eddy. Listen. Do you know where Dad is?'

'Eat my shorts. Over and out.'

'Concentrate! This is important. Are we going the right way to find him?'

'Right way,' yelled Eddy from the roof rack. 'Right way. Over and out!'

'Driving round in this part of the forest is so frustrating,' said Mum in a weary voice. 'It's not in our area and I haven't got a proper map, and according to the map I *have* got, this road doesn't exist.'

'Give me a look.' Meg pored over the map as Mum kept grimly driving.

'Squawk!'

Eddy suddenly tapped on Mark's window with his beak, demanding to be let in, because he'd nearly got swiped off the roof rack by an overhanging branch.

'No smart remarks from you,' said Mum. 'I'm not in the mood.'

'No smart remarks,' Eddy agreed amiably. 'Suck snails. Don't pop ya top.'

Mum slowed the car to a crawl as they peered out.

'There's an old track here,' said Meg, pointing at the map. 'I reckon someone's blocked off the entrance from Number 3 and then widened it a bit near the crossroads with that clearing where Dad's van was parked. That's so most people take the left hand fork if they accidentally come across it. See? According to this map the track runs round in a sort of circle and comes out on the Mount Sabine road near Dean's Marsh.'

Alice, who had her head stuck out the window to avoid that cocky's breath, which smelt like rotten sunflower seeds, suddenly stiffened and gave an excited yelp.

'What is it, girl?' asked Mike anxiously, as she yelped more loudly and began to wag her tail.

'It's not the enemy or she'd be baring her teeth and growling,' said Boris. 'I'll try and get a thought picture. I'll just—'

But before he could attempt to tune in, Alice leapt straight out the window and went rushing off into the bush.

'If she's chasing a rabbit,' said Mum, stopping the car, 'I'll tie her up for a week. And no juicy bones either! She'll be on dry food and water!'

'I don't think it's a rabbit.' Mike looked anxious.

'I reckon she's found something, all right,'

said Boris, as Alice barked her head off in the undergrowth.

'Let's party. Over and out,' squawked Eddy, and swift as a bunch of white feathers on an arrow head, he swooped off after Alice.

'Talk about do a disappearing act,' said Mark crossly. 'Maybe he belongs to a magician or something.'

'Well, if he does, I hope Eddy can conjure up Dad!' Meg sounded worried.

Boris sighed. 'We'd better investigate.'

'I hope,' said Mum, looking grim, 'we *do* find your father at the end of this wild cocky and dog chase, because I'm getting very, *very* worried!'

Eight

Following Alice's excited yapping should've been easy but it wasn't, because thick black-berry bushes grew among the gums in this part of the forest, the long barbed canes scratching them and tearing at their clothes.

'How could someone've been dragged in here?' Meg puzzled aloud as a particularly nasty barb ripped at her face.

'There are other offshoot tracks,' Mike pointed out. 'Alice probably scented Dad and took the shortest route through this tangle to another track.'

'The shortest route for a *dog*, not a *human*! Boris, can you go back to the wagon and find my old gardening shears? I wish I'd brought the brushcutter, but I didn't think we'd been bush-bashing like this.'

'I'll go with him,' said Meg. 'There might be something else we could use. What about the car jack?'

'Bring *anything*,' said Mum.

'Do you mean we can gun the wagon and ram it into the blackberries?' asked Mark, his face lighting up at the thought of smashing down blackberry bushes with Mum's new car.

'In your dreams,' said Boris, as Mum looked grim. 'Come on, Mark. You can help carry something.'

'I'll try the mobile again,' said Mum, as she wiped the sweat off her face. She was obviously feeling frustrated. They'd only progressed a few metres. Of course Alice, being low-slung, and with her loose, thick coat, could wriggle through dense scrub, even though she couldn't quite manage blackberry thickets. In the distance Mum could hear the big dog barking sharply. Flinching as she dialled, she prayed that Alice hadn't cornered a tiger snake. Or worse, that Dad hadn't been bitten by one. What on earth was going on? This trip in the Otways seemed to be turning into a jungle hunt for heaven knew what, and it was getting more like hell than heaven by the minute!

Suddenly the Aussie Angels with Mark in tow came crashing through the undergrowth wearing triumphant grins on their faces.

Mark had the shears. Meg had a spade. And, to Mum's delight, Boris and Mike had the heavy-duty brushcutter and also a small can of fuel. Mum had forgotten that she'd been attacking brambles with it near the creek a few weeks ago and left the brushcutter under a rug while she went into town to buy some groceries. Because it was hidden, she'd completely forgotten it was there.

'We can use all of these things,' said Meg,

handing Mum her ear muffs, gloves and goggles. 'Especially the brushcutter. I hope the environmentalists don't mind us hacking through the scrub, but this is an emergency.'

'Blackberries are a noxious plant and so's mistletoe,' said Mum, impatiently brushing an overhanging strand from her hair as she put on her goggles to protect her eyes from flying twigs and thorns. 'So we're doing the gum trees and other native fauna a big favour. Let's go.'

Mike and Meg had been given lessons in operating the brushcutter, so Mum didn't have to do all the hard work. Because Boris and Mark hadn't, they had to use the shears and the spade to clear away the prickly runners from the path that Mike proceeded to make.

Operating a brushcutter was hard work because it was a heavy piece of machinery. There was a harness to wear but you had to lean forward, keeping your body and legs out of the way as much as possible just in case it hit a rock or something. Dad had taught the twins always to treat the brushcutter and other equipment like axes and chainsaws and electric shears with great respect.

Most mothers wouldn't be able to work a brushcutter, thought Boris admiringly as he watched this one slice through the blackberries, cutting a narrow path so they could walk in single file after her.

Every now and then Mum stopped to listen. Meg had her compass out to pinpoint the direction of Alice's yelping, which was becoming more frantic.

How did she get into the bush so far and so quickly? Meg shook her head as she took the brushcutter from Mum and leaned it against a tree while she put on the harness.

But there was no need to cut any further, because with the next sweeping slice at the blackberries, they were suddenly in a small clearing, and there was a path leading away into the bush.

'A kangaroo track,' said Mike. 'But it'll do us. Maybe this's what Alice found further back near the road when she jumped out of the window. She's followed the scent of the roos and found the track easily.'

'Pity we don't have such a strong sense of smell,' Meg said ruefully as she rested the brushcutter on the ground. 'It would have saved us all that time crashing round in the scrub.'

'Will we carry this stuff or leave it behind a tree?' asked Mike.

'Leave it,' said Mum. 'It's too heavy.'

'But bring the brushcutter,' said Mark, who was secretly hoping that they'd all get worn out working it and give him a go.

'No. We'll take the spade and the ruck-sacks,' said Mum.

'But we might need the brushcutter to chop the poachers' legs off,' argued Mark. 'It'll be our weapon of destruction if we have to rescue Dad.'

'Sure. The poachers are really gunna stand still and let you slice their legs off,' said Mike. 'When are you going to grow up?'

Boris gave Mark's arm an understanding squeeze. When he'd been Mark's age he would've sliced up a whole city with a brush-cutter. But now, of course, thanks to the Green family and Carol the camel, he was a different boy.

'Violence doesn't work, mate,' he said. 'Sometimes you've got to fight cunning with *more* cunning!'

'Like this?' Mark dragged a homemade slingshot from his pocket.

'Mark!' Mum was horrified. 'Where did you get that?'

'I swapped it for a bunch of footy cards with Ricky Valdani at school,' said Mark defiantly. 'He said it was a fair swap. *He* said—'

'I don't care what he said! You know you're not allowed to have anything that can cause harm to someone or some*thing*. Now, give it to me and...'

An agonised howling cut through the air like a sword, making everyone jump.

'Let's go,' yelled Mike, and went rushing

down the path with the others charging behind him. Boris ran fast and dragged the spade behind him.

Meg ripped along with her rucksack bouncing on her back, and Mum and Mark brought up the rear. The overhanging bushes meant that sometimes they had to run doubled over, and in one place they had to crawl under a fallen log. They'd never been in this part of the Otways before either, and although the growth was familiar, the terrain wasn't. Without the compass and the fact that they'd hacked a trail through the densest parts, they'd never find the way back to Mum's wagon if it got dark, because all the trees and scrub started to look the same, and it was so easy to lose all sense of direction in the bush.

But of course they had Alice's yelping and barking to guide them along, so when they got there and found out what was causing her to go demented, she could lead them out again by a shorter route. That is, if she wasn't injured. Or if she'd found Dad, and *he* hadn't been injured!

'We're coming, Alice,' bellowed Mark, as he closed in on her frantic barking.

'Quiet!' hissed Mike. 'The poachers might be there and hear you.'

'I'll go back for the brushcutter then.'

'You'll keep your mouth shut and do as you're told,' snapped Mum, surprising everybody, because Mum never told kids to keep their mouths shut! She was really uptight.

Scrambling, bending low, then trying to run whenever they could, the Angels, Mum and Mark pushed their way deeper into the forest as Alice continued to bark and howl.

'Move it and groove it,' shouted a raucous voice as they rounded a bend. 'Burger with the lot. Shut ya trap. Give us a kiss.'

'Eddy,' screeched Mark, darting forward.

But the others weren't worrying about Eddy, or even Alice bounding round and round in circles and barking her head off.

Lying in a ditch with his wrists and ankles tightly bound, his face into the ground and half covered by bushes, was Dad.

Maybe he was dead.

Nine

One of the best things going for the Green family was Mum's experience as a nurse, so she moved quickly.

'Cut the cords,' she instructed, as she bent to check Dad's pulse and felt deftly round his windpipe where Meg knew one of the two main arteries were located.

They could all see the gaping hole near his shoulder where someone had shot him. Blood seeped out in an ominous red pool.

Swiftly Mike cut the tight cords with a pair

of surgical scissors from the first aid kit. This was certainly one time he was glad that the Angels had their rucksacks with all their supplies. Mum ran her hands lightly over Dad, checking for any broken bones before she rolled him gently onto his side.

'CPR?' asked Boris quietly.

'No. He's breathing,' said Mum. 'But it's very shallow. He's lost a lot of blood.'

Meg shuddered and struggled not to scream. Someone who was prepared to shoot a human being, especially a forest ranger with full government authority to apprehend poachers and shooters, wasn't going to be too fussy about firing at a woman deep in the forest with only a bunch of kids, a dog and a cocky.

'Get the ambo. Get the ambo,' said Eddy with his head on one side, gazing at Dad from Mark's shoulder. He made a soft siren sound in his throat. 'Oooo ah, ooooo ah, oooo ah.'

'We would if we could, mate,' said Boris, as Meg helped Mum clean the wound as well as they could and bind it tightly to control the bleeding.

'It's missed his heart,' said Mum, her training keeping her calm. 'But the bullet's still in there. This isn't good.'

'What are we going to do?' asked Mark, clinging to Mum's back like a frightened koala.

'It's okay, matey,' said Meg, putting her arms round him. 'Dad's got help now, and Mum knows what to do, so it'll be all right.'

Mark allowed Meg to cuddle him, then he pushed her away. The other boys weren't acting sooky, and neither was Meg, so he had to be brave.

'We'd better fire off one of those flares,' said Mum.

'What if the killers see it?'

'That's too bad. Fire one, just in case someone's around and reports it to the police. We'll save the other one just in case things get worse.'

Though how much worse they could get she wasn't sure.

Mike got out a flare and carefully set it up away from the group. He set it off and it shot high into the air, leaving a trail of red smoke. But how visible was it when they were somewhere in the middle of a mountain range?

'You dad couldn't have crawled here tied up the way he was,' said Boris, who was peering at the ground. 'There has to be a track somewhere nearby, wide enough for a car or a van. They've dragged him from a vehicle. Ah. See? There's the marks.'

He pointed to where the earth had been scuffed and marks could be seen where an object had been dragged along. And that object was Dad! There were even splotches of blood on some of the leaves.

'I wonder if they shot him near his van then drove here to dump him?' asked Boris.

'I reckon that's what happened. They didn't count on us finding him so quickly.'

Meg started to cry. It was awful seeing her father unconscious and so white. Mark bit his bottom lip hard. The other boys weren't crying so he had to hold back his tears. Then he saw rough, tough Boris wipe his sleeve across his face and realised that Boris was crying too. So Mark burst into tears all over Dad.

Dad groaned and moved his head slightly.

'Lie still, dear,' said Mum, nodding at Meg to pass the water container in case he wanted a small drink. After all, he didn't need dehydration to add to his complications.

But Dad lapsed back into unconsciousness. Mum frowned. This wasn't good at all, but she didn't want to frighten everyone, so she told them to empty a rucksack and roll it up to put under his head, and place the blanket that they always carried over him because, although the sun was shining brightly, the air was cool here under the trees and the ground was damp. She wanted to put the other space blanket under him but was reluctant to do so in case any movement started up the bleeding again.

'Here's a track,' called Mike. He'd gone exploring. 'It's wide enough to drive down too. It looks like a forestry one, not used much, but there's definitely been someone driving on it recently because the grass is all flattened.'

Meg looked at her compass. 'It must lead back to Dad's van,' she said, as Mike returned.

'If Alice hadn't panicked and jumped out the window we could've *driven* here,' said Mark crossly, and he glared at Alice, who hung her head.

Boris picked up her doggy thought picture immediately.

'She caught Dad's scent in the breeze and thought she was doing the right thing,' he explained. 'Of course she was able to run straight here, directly as the crow flies, as my Gran would say, from point A to point B. But we had no idea where to go, except to try and follow her barking, so we ended up bashing through the bush in a big circle instead of strolling along the road a few metres and finding the track which led here. Alice thought she was doing a good job.'

'Sorry, Alice,' said Mark, giving her a big hug.

'Sorry, sorry,' echoed Eddy, and hopped onto Alice's head.

Mum looked at the Angels. 'Your father's in a bad way and we need urgent help,' she said quietly. 'I don't want to leave him, but I think I'll have to do it, because our only option is to get the wagon or the van, whichever is the closest, and bring it here. I've got a spare set of keys for the van here in my bag. But it's dangerous, because these people are desperate and could shoot you if they come back.'

'I'll do it,' said Boris.

'YOU?'

Boris shrugged. 'I could drive a car when I was nine,' he said with a trace of pride. 'And last year I drove the getaway car when Brendan was shot in the foot during an armed hold-up.'

'You didn't tell us that!' Meg was shocked.

'It's not something I'm proud of: he made me do it.'

'Okay, you're underage, but you can drive and that's the skill we need right now,' said

Mum, nodding at Boris, who suddenly looked pleased.

Being one of the Boola Boys with brothers who were always in and out of jail had a certain status, but with the wrong crowd. Secretly Boris had been scared of his brothers. And of his drunken father. They were a bad lot. So he knew he'd never get involved in crime no matter how much someone offered him. And any driving he did when he was an adult certainly wouldn't be in a getaway car!

Mum dug round in her bag for the keys.

'I was thinking,' said Mike, passing them to Boris. 'Eddy is one very smart bird.'

Eddy put his crest up and down twice to show that he liked the compliment.

'What's your plan?' asked Meg. She knew her brother inside out, and he seldom wasted words or thoughts on frivolous things.

'We can write a note and tie it to Eddy's leg. With a bit of luck Boris can give Eddy a thought picture to fly straight to Animal Haven so that Annie can alert the ambulance and police.'

'Like a carrier pigeon,' said Mark excitedly.

'Suck ya socks. Eat dirt. You're a pooh box,' said Eddy, looking annoyed.

Pigeons were common, dull-looking and dumb birds. Of course Eddy had only ever met a few wood pigeons in the bush that spent their time cooing and pooing, so there could be some super smart ones round, but...

'Stop thinking about pigeons and *concentrate*,' said Boris sternly. 'You're on a carrier *mission*. Right now it isn't important whether you're a pigeon, a cocky, an eagle or a jumbo jet as long as you get there in a hurry.'

He thought up a picture of Uncle Pete and his van too, just in case he was rambling round in the Otways looking for them, while Meg scribbled a note.

"EMERGENCY. DAD SHOT, LOSING BLOOD FAST. SEND AMBULANCE AND POLICE TO..." She paused. 'Where are we?'

'That's the problem,' said Mum. 'I'm not

sure. I think we're at the back of the Mount Sabine road somewhere.'

'That's too vague.'

'Put, "FOLLOW THE COCKY",' said Mark. 'Eddy knows where we are and he won't get lost, will you Eddy?'

'That's a good idea,' replied Boris. 'Eddy, fly low so they can see you, okay? You might have to be patient and double back to lead them here. But we're relying on you.'

'The reward is a whole packet of Tim Tams,' said Mum without looking up from Dad, as Meg crossed out "TO" and wrote "FOLLOW THE COCKY".

Eddy preened, puffed out his chest, and elevated his crest so that it stood up off his head like a sunflower on steroids. As far as *he* was concerned, Eddy the cocky was an Angel too now!

Alice huffed silently and sulked. *She'd* led them to Dad. Without her barking till her throat felt like it was on fire, they'd never have got here. Where was *her* reward?

'Alice,' said Boris, reading her thoughts, 'you'd better come with me. I need a protector and I need a quick guide to take me the shortest route to one of the vehicles, okay? Now, let's go.'

Mum looked up from rubbing Dad's chafed wrists. 'Take Mike with you,' she said. 'You might need extra help. Meg and Mark can stay here with me.'

Eddy gave Mark a quick farewell peck on the cheek.

'Take care, Eddy,' said Mark, looking worried. 'And if anyone shoots at you, *duck*!'

'Bombs away,' said Eddy. 'Over and out.'

He launched himself into the air with the note firmly attached to his leg by Meg's elastic hair band and went winging away towards the south east.

'I hope he knows where he's going,' said Meg anxiously.

'He does. He's one smart bird.'

'Mum, are you going to be okay here?' Mike bit his lip. He didn't want to leave them alone, yet they had to get help, and the boys needed Alice and her super-nose to go with them.

'Anyone tries to hurt us and I'll dong them with the spade,' said Meg with false cheerfulness.

'And I'll hit 'em between the eyes with my slingshot,' added Mark.

Mum didn't say anything. Maybe she was glad that he had it, but secretly Mark was really scared that he might have to use it, because he was the only one left to defend Dad, Mum and Meg.

Dad started moaning softly.

'He's regaining consciousness,' said Mum.

But maybe that wasn't such a good thing, when they were stuck out in the middle of the bush with hardly any medical supplies and easy targets for people who would probably stop at nothing to get rid of them?

Ten

'Who did this to you?' asked Mum gently when Dad struggled to focus on her concerned face.

'I don't know,' he mumbled. 'I found their operation. Bird poachers. Someone shot me from behind. I didn't hear them coming.'

And he was unconscious again.

'You'd better get going,' said Meg, as Mum bent over Dad. 'This is life or death.'

Boris, Mike and Alice dashed off. When they reached the main track, Boris took off his red cap and hung it on a branch to mark the spot.

'Who knows, we mightn't be able to find this place again,' he said solemnly.

'What if you get sunstroke?' asked Mike anxiously.

'I won't. I've got thick hair and the sun's not that fierce today. Anyway there's plenty of shade from these trees.'

The big dog loped along easily beside them. She was feeling important because she knew the way to Dad's patrol van, which was actually much closer than Mum's wagon. Humans were weird. All they had to do was get down on all fours and use their noses when the situation got tricky.

And another thing: they didn't seem to like having a good scratch, they didn't like rolling on their backs with their legs in the air, they peed in toilets and not in the garden, and they didn't enjoy a nice juicy bone that had been left to go lovely and ripe in a shallow earthy hole. Without her, the Greens could never survive.

'That's right, Alice,' puffed Boris, as they ran up a steep hill. 'We humans need you dogs to sort us out.'

'Huh?' Mike gaped at Boris. Then he just grinned to himself. He wished that he could do this thought picture thing too. Boris was trying to teach him, but it was hard because he kept thinking in words. And of course animals didn't understand words unless they were spoken out loud!

'This is a bit better,' said Mike as they legged it downhill.

'Harder on the calves, though.'

They stopped talking and used their energy for running. Alice was in the lead now. She knew that Dad's patrol van was just round the next bend. Triumphantly she rounded the corner then stopped so suddenly that Boris crashed into her.

The van had disappeared!

Alice looked round. What was going on?

This was definitely the place! Well, lots of bends in the bush looked the same. So maybe she'd made a mistake.

Then her nose got busy, sniffing the ground. Yes, this *was* where the van had been. But someone had moved it.

'What's wrong, Alice?'

Boris squatted to have a thought conversation. Then he looked at Mike.

'Alice knows that the van's been moved,' he explained.

'So why didn't we hear the engine start up?'

'Keep your voice down. Maybe they moved it when we were brushcutting before, so we didn't hear the engine.'

'Hmm.'

Nose to the ground, Alice was following something off the track.

'Come out of there. You could tread on a tiger snake,' snapped Mike.

Alice suddenly bolted out, knocking over several stout bushes.

'How did she...?'

'They've been chopped down then put back to conceal the tracks,' whispered Mike excitedly. 'Look. Here's the tyre marks. The van's been driven into the scrub.' He was starting to feel scared. What if the poachers were lying in wait for them? What if they shot Alice and then *them* too?

'What do we do now?' Boris was looking nervous. Once when he'd tried to rescue Alice from his brother, he'd been shot, and it had hurt. He wasn't too keen to cop another bullet.

'We'd better follow.'

'I guess that's the best thing.' Boris wasn't sure.

Mike wasn't too sure either. 'I hope they didn't drive the van too far into the bush. It's taking us further away from the others. And maybe it's a trap.'

'Well, standing here talking isn't going to solve the puzzle and we have to know what's happened.'

It was easy to follow the van's passage through the scrub, and it didn't take long to find out where it was either, because suddenly they came abruptly to a steep drop.

'Careful,' warned Mike, as Boris nearly lost his balance on the damp leaf mould underfoot.

Cautiously, while Alice made little moaning noises, they lay on their tummies and peered over.

'I can't see...'

'There. You can just catch the glint of the sun on metal or glass.'

At the very bottom of the cliff was the upturned van, almost totally hidden by the thick scrub. Due to the overhanging cliff face on both sides and the steep terrain, it would be difficult for anyone to notice it from a helicopter and almost impossible to track it from the ground. Even if someone searched with infra-red cameras the rocks would screen it.

'I'll pinpoint it on my compass,' said Mike. 'Then later a team can come and get all the stuff out.'

The van was fitted out with a special stretcher and all sorts of first aid gear as well as special tools and equipment for rescuing animals. There was also the expensive radio and other things that needed to be retrieved.

The police would probably need to take photos as well to be used in evidence.

But there wasn't time to think about all that now. They had to get to Mum's wagon.

'Just as well she gave us the keys to both,' said Mike. 'And let's hope the wagon's not too far from here.'

'You did a good job, Alice,' said Boris, squatting on his heels and gazing at the dog. 'You found the van. But now we need to find Mum's car. And fast.'

Alice turned round and went to dash through the scrub.

'No. Wait. We can't follow you. You're a dog!'

Alice came back, and if dogs could look impatient, she was. She brushed past the two boys and went pounding back the way they'd come.

'She's not messing about,' said Boris, as they

sprinted after her, trying not to trip over branches and catch their feet in the flattened but tangled undergrowth.

'Why couldn't all this be happening in the desert?' panted Mike. 'I reckon it'd be much easier running through sand.'

'Specially with Carol. Doing the hard yards with Alice isn't exactly a picnic.'

By now they were on the track and the going was more straightforward. Alice was racing ahead with her ears back, determined to find Mum's car and earn that juicy bone. A packet of Tim Tams indeed, and just because that cocky could fly and she couldn't! Well, she'd show them.

Ooops. Near disaster! She skidded to a halt just short of sudden death and started barking.

The boys heard her and looked at each other as they pounded down the track.

'Oh, no. *Now* what?' puffed Mike.

'I dunno. This is starting to feel like *Indiana Jones and the Temple of Doom,* except there's no temple,' said Boris.

They rounded the next bend and found Alice bailed up against a big tree with a large and angry tiger snake poised to strike. It had been snoozing on the track in the sun, hard to see because its stripes were a defined golden colour, almost the colour of the yellow clay of the track, against its dark scales. And it was a big one too. One bite from those fangs and Alice would be a dead dog within an hour.

'Stay still, Alice,' warned Mike, as they slowed to a walk. 'Don't move.'

Alice had met a few snakes in her travels and had even killed one or two small ones, but this was the granddaddy of all snakes. She kept her eyes on its weaving head. If it lunged, she wasn't going to be a heroine; she was outa there. Fast.

Cautiously Mike pulled off his cap and approached the snake, which was now swaying back and forward, looking first at them and then at the dog. He tossed the cap on the ground near it.

Zap. It struck savagely, its powerful fangs

full of venom sinking into the cap again and again.

Boris sent a thought picture, quick as a flash. 'Behind the tree and then round to me, Alice. NOW.'

For once Alice did as she was told. Because it was spring there was sure to be a female snake and babies nearby. The best idea right now was to get out while the going was good. The snake stared at the cap. It could stay there for an hour gazing at it, or it could change its mind and go for them. They weren't taking any chances.

'Let's go,' said Mike, and giving the snake a wide berth, they continued down the road.

'All we need is an armoured tank with guns blazing to come charging round the next bend,' said Boris, trying to lighten the moment. 'This is starting to get stupid. If it wasn't so real I'd almost think we were on a movie set or candid camera or something.'

'Yeah. How could anyone think the Australian bush is boring!'

Alice yelped and Mike jumped.

'*What?*'

'It's okay. She's just telling you that she's spotted the wagon.'

It was parked where Mum had left it and as they got closer they could see it was still locked and not interfered with at all. Obviously the poachers hadn't gone this way or, if they had, they'd left it alone, thinking it belonged to bushwalkers or tourists.

'Okay, here we go. Just as well it's an automatic,' said Boris, once they were safely inside. 'I don't think I could drive one of those old four-on-the-floor jobs.'

Carefully he drove it along the main track and onto the branching track which led to Dad, Mum and the others.

'It was simple. If we'd kept going along here in the first place we would've got to Dad much sooner,' said Mike crossly, as Boris tried to steer and control the wagon's speed at the same time.

Alice looked dejected.

'Yeah, but we'd have missed the bit where

they dragged him into the scrub,' said Boris. 'Without Alice's nose we'd never have found him till it was too late.

Alice brightened up.

'How much further?'

'I don't think it's far now. Start looking for my red cap.'

'There it is!'

Mike pointed. The red cap stood out among all the green foliage. Boris immediately slowed down.

Should he toot the horn to let the others know they were coming? No, that might alert the poachers if they were lurking about.

'Come on,' he said, taking the keys out of the ignition. 'Let's hope—'

'We're not too late,' Mike finished the sentence for him, as they pushed their way after an eager Alice and into the scrub.

Eleven

Dad was actually sitting up, propped against a tree, because it was easier for him to breathe. He was conscious and Mum had given him pain killers from the first aid kit. He looked so pale and tired.

'Can you go and get the car rug?' Mum asked, when they told her how Dad's patrol van had been pushed over the cliff. 'And leave the rear doors open with any clothing or cushions in the middle to make a soft bed.'

Unfortunately the special stretcher was in

the patrol van along with all the other equipment, so the car rug would have to be used like a stretcher.

'I hope this doesn't jolt you round too much,' Mum said to Dad anxiously, as they laid him down on it.

Everyone took an edge and when Mum said "lift" they all did. Even Alice had a piece of the rug in her teeth. Luckily Dad wasn't heavy, but even so it was hard work carrying him to the wagon as gently as they could. Somehow they managed to get him inside. He groaned once and then he was silent.

'Is he okay?' asked Mark, looking scared.

'Yes. He's just conserving energy,' said Mum calmly as they all piled in and she started the engine.

'You know, this is like something out of a *Die Hard* movie,' said Mike from the rear where he was minding Dad and trying to stop him moving about too much. 'It's—unbelievable.'

'I keep pinching myself to see if it's a bad dream,' murmured Meg.

'Poachers with guns! Someone shooting your father and pushing his van over a cliff!' said Mum. 'I guess the bad guys have come to the Otways. You see this stuff on TV but you don't think it's real till it happens to you.'

'The bad guys were *always* here,' said Boris.

Everyone was quiet. They were all thinking the same thing. Was one or more of his brothers involved? A couple of them were out of jail, but Boris had told them he thought they were in Queensland.

'Mum, is Dad gunna die?' squeaked Mark, suddenly voicing everyone's fears.

'I don't think so,' Mum replied. 'He's a tough nut to crack. I think he'll be right once we get him to hospital and he gets some more blood into him. I think I've stopped the flow now, but it's left him very weak.'

'This track seems to go forever.' Meg screwed up her face as she peered at the map.

'Would it be quicker to turn right at this fork, Mum? See?' She pointed to the broken lines which indicated a bush track. 'If this is our position, then this track joins up with the Benwerrin Road and takes us into the other road that ends up at Boyer.'

'But what if we're not actually on this track?' Boris jabbed his finger on another part of the map. 'What if we're *here* instead?'

Meg sighed. 'According to my compass, we came in from that direction, but it's so hard to be sure of the direction with the tracks criss-crossing all the time.'

'Try the mobile again,' said Mum.

But there was only a buzzing noise. They were still too low in the hills to pick up a satellite signal.

'Wait. Isn't that—?'

'Eddy!' yelled Mark.

'Shh, you'll disturb Dad!'

'Oops, sorry. But it *is* Eddy and—here he comes.'

Mark ducked as the cocky swooped cheekily into the wagon and perched on his shoulder.

'Whirly bird. Whirly bird,' he squawked,

flapping his wings and putting his crest up and down furiously. 'Over and out.'

'What's he talking about? Whirly bird? What's a whirly bird, his girlfriend or something?'

'I think—it *is*! It's a helicopter. I can hear it,' said Meg. 'Listen.'

Mum pulled the car off to the side of the track.

'Get out and wave to attract attention,' she ordered. 'Anything bright. Jump up and down. Move about.'

'We're here,' bellowed Mark, leaping up and down like he was standing on a bullants' nest. 'Yoo hoo, guys. Come and get us!'

'They can't hear you,' said Meg. 'You might as well stop yelling and put energy into waving.'

'They've seen us,' called Boris, as the co-pilot waved. Then, 'Oh. NO! They're going away. Come back! *Come back!*'

'They can't land on this track. It's not wide enough,' said Mum. 'I think I'd better follow them. From the air they'll be able to spot a clearing. Everyone, keep an eye on where that 'copter lands, will you, while I concentrate on driving?'

Mum drove slowly along the track while Boris and Meg ran ahead with Alice, and Mike and Mark put their heads out the window.

Suddenly Eddy, who'd been perched on the roof rack, gave a shrill squawk that nearly pierced everyone's ear drums.

'Going down,' he shrieked. 'Going down. Down down down.'

'The 'copter's landing. See? Look at the dust.'

'It's not far. There must be a clearing,' panted Meg as Mum drew level.

Mike was still in the rear with Dad.

'Dad's still breathing but he doesn't look too good, Mum,' he called softly.

Mum swung the wagon round the bend. Immediately they could see the helicopter land like a black moth in the clearing and two men climb out and duck under the still whirring blades. One was Dr Barclay, and the other was Johnny the pilot, whom they all knew, because his daughter Katie was the one who kept passing Mike love notes and chocolate bars on the school bus.

Driving right up, Mum turned off the ignition and got out as the men hurried to open the rear door.

They had been to lots of emergencies and knew exactly what to do. So Dad was soon on a stretcher and loaded into the helicopter.

'Will he be all right?' asked Mum anxiously. 'I can't go too. I have to stay with the children and drive them home.'

'He'll be fine. When you've taken the kids home, come into the hospital and things will be more stable, okay?'

'Thank you,' said Mum. 'There's just one other thing. How did you find us so quickly?'

'Followed that pesky cocky,' grinned Johnny, as he swung into the pilot's seat. 'Annie called us straight away: we flew to Animal

Haven to get more directions, and this cocky led us to you.'

'Cocky wants a Tim Tam,' said Eddy firmly. 'Read my lips. Over and out.'

'You haven't got lips, Eddy,' said Mark, stroking the shiny white feathers, 'but don't worry. You can have all the Tim Tams in the world. Can't he, Mum?'

Eddy looked excited at this news. All the Tim Tams in the world? He could live in luxury for the rest of his life. He flew onto the roof rack and his crest popped up and down like a Jack-in-the-box. Tim Tams? He was ready to go home!

'I don't know about all the Tim Tams in the world,' said Mum with a tired smile, 'but Eddy can definitely have the packet of Tim Tams in the pantry, and that's a promise!'

Suddenly there was the sound of another helicopter approaching. This time they could see it was a black and white one, much larger, with POLICE written on the side.

'Get back,' yelled the pilot. 'It can kick up stones and stuff when it lands.'

They quickly got out of the way as the helicopter came down into the clearing.

As soon as it landed, several police officers spilled out and ran, bent double, under the rotating blades.

'Someone reported an emergency flare being set off in this area,' said one of them, as another went over to talk to the pilot of the first helicopter and two other officers stood by ready for action. 'Know anything about it?'

'That was us,' said Mum. 'My husband's the ranger from Animal Haven and he's been shot by poachers. Well, we think that's what's happened. The children have told me that his patrol van's been pushed over a cliff near here somewhere too. Now he's just about to be airlifted to hospital.'

The black helicopter rose in the air as she spoke and went winging away into the sky. With that, Mum burst into tears. The Angels were shocked because they'd hardly ever seen her cry. She was usually so strong and resilient, and to see her crumple in a heap was scary.

Mark immediately started bawling his eyes out too, and he clung to Mum like a limpet to a rock.

That seemed to make her pull herself together. 'It's okay, son,' she said through her tears as she stroked his head. 'It's okay. It was just a bit too much, that's all.'

'You've had a tough time,' said another police officer. 'Are you able to drive? Do you want us to take a couple of the kids back with us and one of the officers can accompany you? Or do you want us to drop you at the hospital and one of us can drive the kids back?'

'I don't know,' said Mum. 'I can't think straight. Maybe I should go straight to the hospital if you can drop me there.'

'Hang on. What about these killers?' said Mark to the biggest police officer. 'Aren't you going to find them and shoot them?'

'Don't worry, son.' The police officer put a hand on his shoulder. 'There'll be a team out here soon to investigate the scene of the crime. We'll catch them, you just wait and see. Now, is there anything else we can help you with?'

'Yes,' said Mark. 'Our brushcutter and stuff. It's in there somewhere.' He pointed into the bush. 'There's no way those killers are getting our brushcutter. They'd probably go round cutting everybody into bits.'

The police officer tried not to laugh. He put on a serious face as he knelt down so that his eyes were on the same level as Mark's.

'We'll get your brushcutter and the other stuff,' he promised. 'But right now, would you like to come for a ride in the helicopter with your mum?'

'Can Mike and Meg and Boris and Eddy come too?' Mark's eyes lit up like twin stars.

The police officer ticked them off on his fingers. 'That's six. Even if two officers go in the wagon, that'll be a squeeze. We can only take one adult and three kids maximum. Sorry.'

'Eddy doesn't take up much room. He's a cocky,' Mark explained.

'Pick ya nose. Take me to ya leader. Over and out,' said Eddy, flying onto Mark's shoulder and looking at the police officer with his head on one side.

Even he knew that helicopters were faster than cars, and if he could get to those Tim Tams in double quick time, that suited him just fine!

Twelve

Two of the police officers went in the wagon with Boris and Alice. Boris said he didn't mind going back to Animal Haven by road because he'd already been in a helicopter before, and he didn't think it was fair that Alice, who'd done such a good job, should have to travel with strangers, even if they were the police!

'Are you sure?' Mum had looked relieved.

She'd just wanted to see the kids dropped off safely at Animal Haven before the police helicopter took her into the hospital to see Dad.

Boris was perfectly happy to travel with the cops. Secretly he'd decided that he wouldn't mind being one when he grew up. And if he didn't end up a cop, he'd like to work with animals.

He leaned over the back of the seat and fired questions at them the whole way back to Animal Haven. What was it like going to the police academy? Would it be better to be a detective or a straight-out cop? What about the water police? Was that better than ordinary cop work and how did you get to be one? Or the mounted police, and had anyone considered using a mounted camel?

Luckily the two police officers were friendly and didn't mind answering the barrage of questions that he fired at them.

'A mounted camel?' one said. 'Now there's a good idea!'

Boris sat back, doing calculations in his

head. If he could join the police force and take Carol with him, life would be perfect!

The way back was straightforward because the police knew the area rather well, since it was often under aerial surveillance due to certain criminal types doing their gardening in the area. The driver took a left turn onto the Mount Sabine Road and another left when he came to the Kennet Track. It seemed so easy once they were out of the maze of bush tracks in the middle of the forest.

'I'll give you a lead,' said Boris. 'I reckon one of the footprints belonged to this kid I know. I used to be in the School Rulers gang, but I quit to go straight because I wanted to be an Angel.'

'I see,' said the driver. He glanced across at his mate as if to ask what on earth this kid was raving about!

'What makes you think you recognised a footprint and its owner?' said the other officer.

'Because Greash wears these special runners. No one else does because they cost heaps. And it looked like his.'

'Greash?'

'His real name's Joel Gargreashi, so we call him Greash.'

'Ah. Gargreashi. Any relation to Nick Gargreashi?'

'That's his dad. And there's Foxie, too. Not that I normally dob or anything, but if they're involved in shooting Mr Green, I'm happy to bust them.'

'Foxie. Is that a sharp-faced kid who looks a bit like a ferret, beady little eyes and a pointy nose? His dad used to knock round with Thomas Boola?'

'Yeah. And Thomas Boola's me brother.'

There was a stunned silence. Then, *'You're one of the Boolas?'*

Alice gave a warning growl deep in her throat. She didn't like the police officer's tone of voice.

'Yeah. But I'm not like my brothers. I told ya, I wanna be a cop and do good stuff, not rob supermarkets and do hold-ups. That's stupid. You only end up shooting people and going to jail. I've got better things to do than that!'

'Ah, I remember now. You're the Boola kid who got shot by his own brother! I heard about it.'

The police officer's voice had changed again. It was sympathetic now, and Alice immediately stopped growling and licked the back of his neck. This was more like it!

The wagon went bumping down the Kennet Track and came out near Old Mill Road. It wasn't far now to Animal Haven. So much had happened in such a short space of time.

When Boris jumped out with Alice, the others were there to greet him.

'Mum phoned from the hospital. Dad's okay and they've operated to get the bullet out and given him some more blood. He's going to be fine.'

'What happened to Uncle Pete?'

'He didn't get the call till late in the

morning and he was busy operating on a race-
horse, so he called the police. But they didn't
know where to search until they saw the flare.
They had police on foot searching in the other
area where we reported the gun shot coming
from, but it turned out that was Old Ben the
hermit shooting a rabbit.'

'So do these poachers get off, then?' Boris
felt the anger swell inside.

'We'll be carrying out a thorough investiga-
tion,' said the police officer. 'Now, if you're
okay, we have to get going.'

'Annie's here,' said Meg. 'And Mum said
she'll be back soon. We're fine.'

Just then Carol came hurtling up at a fast
trot. She flung her furry body at Boris and
nearly knocked him flying.

'Glad to see you too,' said Boris, trying to
maintain his dignity in front of the police
officers. After all, if they were going to vouch
for him when he applied to join the force,
they needed to see that Carol was a dignified
and intelligent animal and not a slobbering,

sentimental sook, which was how she looked right now.

'Cool it Carol,' he said in her ear, trying to send her thought pictures of herself leading the mounted horse patrol in the Moomba parade.

Of course Carol got rather a jumbled message, but since it showed Boris riding her in the front of a heap of horses, she didn't really care that she hadn't picked up the finer details, like he was older and wearing a police uniform!

'Well, Mum'll be here soon, and Annie and Gladys will go home,' said Meg, as a police car turned into the driveway to collect the two officers. 'Annie has to go home. But how we're going to do all the chores and cope without Dad, I don't know.'

'We'll have to work harder,' said Mike, grabbing the slingshot from Mark as he was trying to pot Mum's prize red rose. 'And that includes *you*, you little devil.'

The police waved goodbye as they sped off towards Boyer.

Boris knew what he had to do. The Greens were in trouble and they needed someone to help.

'No dramas,' he said airily, 'I'll come and live here till your dad gets better.'

Underneath his casual offer, his heart was pumping with anxiety. What if they refused him? What if they didn't *want* him?

'Boris, that'd be *excellent*,' cried Meg, throwing her arms round him and giving him a big kiss on the cheek.

Boris went bright red.

'Hubba hubba,' said Mark. 'Love stuff.'

'Hubba hubba. Give us a kiss, darling,' said Eddy, who was perched on the veranda rail to finish his Tim Tam.

Of course they hadn't given him the whole packet at once because he would've been violently ill. One at a time. But he knew the packet was his because Mark had written Eddy on it in black texta, so that emu and that camel could keep their eyes *off his Tim Tams*!

Meg blushed. She and Boris moved away from each other.

'She was just excited, weren't you Meg?' said Mike. 'Don't feel upset, Boris. We need you here.'

'We sure do,' said Meg. 'Sorry. I got a bit carried away. Please stay, Boris, and I promise I won't kiss you any more.'

'Okay,' said Boris, though part of him was thinking he wouldn't really mind being kissed by Meg again. 'We've got heaps of chores, so we'd better get going. But if I could find out who shot your dad, they'd be sorry!'

'We'll keep our eyes and ears open,' said Mike. 'They'll probably go to ground for a while and close their operation down. But once they start up again, we'll be ready. We've got a special ally now. Our eyes in the sky.'

'Yeah. We've got Eddy,' said Mark, forgetting about his slingshot. 'The best in the west!'

'Too right,' said Eddy, pecking up the last crumbs. 'Suck slugs. Over and out!'

Okay Koala

Animal Haven is a temporary home for all sorts of Australian wildlife, although there are a few permanent residents as well, like Oscar the owl, Fur Bag the possum, Cinnamon the koala and Alice the labrador.

Meg and Mike live there too, and they work so hard to help their parents rescue and look after the animals that the locals at Jeff's Creek have nicknamed them the Aussie Angels. Their little brother Mark is more of an Aussie devil, though, and sometimes makes their job difficult with his mischievous tricks. Then there's Boris Boola and his gang...

But koalas are in trouble, and they need rescuing and the Aussie Angels are just the ones for the job!

ISBN 0-7336-1102-8

Whale of a Time

The Aussie Angels, Meg and Mike, are busy again. This time, as well as rescuing an echidna that's been hit by a bike rider and a kangaroo that's been knocked down by a car, they have to save a koala that insists on clinging to a tv antenna. Boris Boola is in big trouble, Elsie the emu has a fight with the clothesline and, of course, that little Aussie devil Mark is running round with a video camera and being no help at all!

Then the whales are in danger of stranding themselves on the beach, and saving them is the hardest job the Angels have ever tackled—until unexpected help comes their way.

Another exciting adventure from one of Australia's best loved writers!

ISBN 0-7336-1099-4

Hello, Possum!

There are lots of brushtail possums at Animal Haven and Fur Bag is the resident mischief maker. But when Ringlet the female ringtail possum is rescued, she needs special care and attention, and the Aussie Angels make sure she gets it. Then another ringtail is rescued from a flooded river and nearly causes a terrible disaster, but Boris Boola, who'd secretly like to be one of the Angels if only he could, and Carol the camel save the day!

ISBN 0-7336-1101-X

Margaret Clark is one of Australia's best loved writers, and her distinctive blend of comedy, sharp observation and commitment has won her readers around the world. Young adult novels including *Back on Track* and *Fat Chance* are contemporary classics, and were inspired by Margaret's many years of working with young people at a drug and alcohol centre; while popular series such as *Hair-Raisers*, *Mango Street* and *Chickabees* have had her fans waiting eagerly for each new book to be published.

These days, Margaret writes books like the *Aussie Angels* series full-time at her house on the south coast of Victoria, which she shares with seven kookaburras, twenty king parrots, two brushtail possums, four koalas, a family of echidnas, a friendly bush rat and many other visitors. She also knows a fantastic secret place in the forest where there are literally millions of glow-worms after dark.